DREAMS ARE MORE REAL THAN BATHTUBS

To Sophie Musgrave Reid
for her wild mind and spirit
with love and thanks
for letting me use some of her words
that helped me write this book
S.M.

To Judy Donner
M-L.G.

Text copyright © 1998 Susan Musgrave
Illustration copyright © 1998 Marie-Louise Gay

Canadian Cataloguing in Publication Data
Musgrave, Susan, 1951 –
Dreams are more real than bathtubs

ISBN 1-55143-107-6

1. Gay, Marie-Louise. II. Title.

PS8576.U7D73 1998   jC813'.54   C98-910398-6
PZ7.M969Dr 1998

Orca Book Publishers gratefully acknowledges the support of our publishing programs provided by the following agencies: the Department of Canadian Heritage, The Canada Council for the Arts, and the British Columbia Arts Council.

Design by Marie-Louise Gay
Typeset by Jim Brennan
Printed and bound in Hong Kong

Orca Book Publishers
PO Box 5626, Station B
Victoria, BC Canada
V8R 6S4

Orca Book Publishers
PO Box 468
Custer, WA   USA
98240-0468

Library of Congress Catalog Card Number: 98-85277

Dreams Are More Real Than Bathtubs

SUSAN MUSGRAVE
MARIE-LOUISE GAY

ORCA BOOK PUBLISHERS

This is
ME
learning to lose my tooth.
This is my old stuffy,
LION.
My sister says he is wearing out,
but he's not.
He's wearing in.

I take Lion on the TRAMPOLINE and shopping for purple shoes but not to the zoo. with me

Even when I go in Grade One, I am taking Lion with me.

I
take
Lion
in
the

BATH

with me.

When he's dried off
I tuck him in bed
and make him be my pillow.

I ask my mum,
"Can I stay up early tonight?"
I don't want to go to sleep
because I get bad dreams.

I don't have any good dreams, mostly just bad ones.

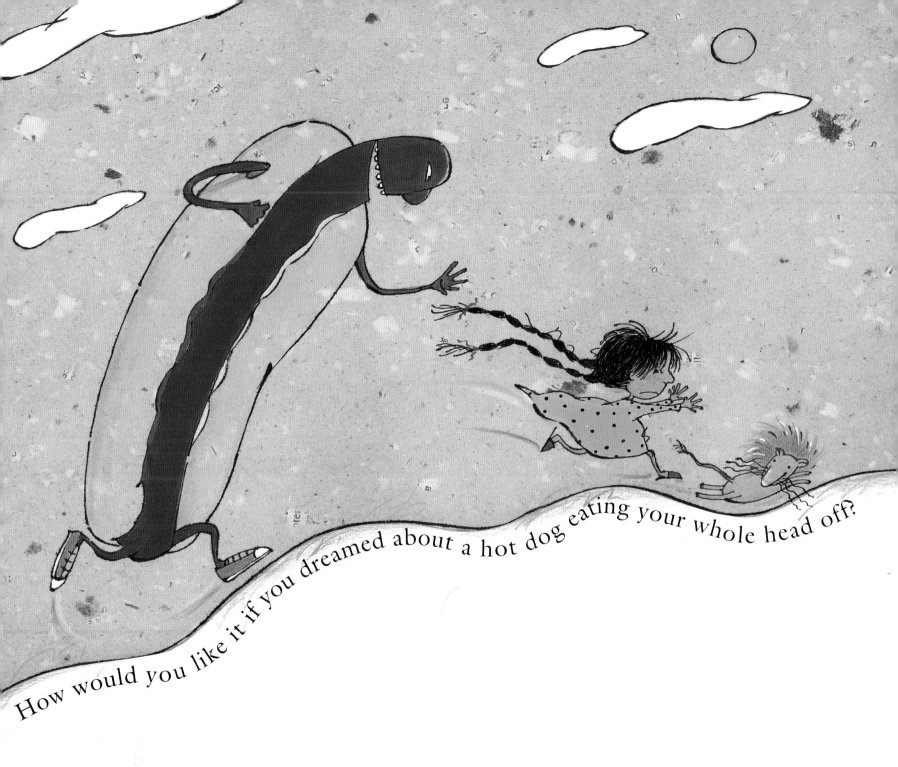

How would you like it if you dreamed about a hot dog eating your whole head off?

My cat
Pine-Cone
wants to stay up early, also.

When I named my cat Pine-Cone
my sister said,

"That's pathetic."

My sister calls Pine-Cone a fleabag
because he likes to scratch.

I tell her, I like getting flea bites, too.
When I itch them it makes me discover different parts
of my body.

At dinnertime I sing,
"Nobody likes me,
everybody hates me,
I'm going in the garden to eat worms."
My sister laughs at me and says,
"Go ahead. Who cares?"

I tell her, when I grow up I want to be a

so I can scare people who laugh at me.
"Pathetic," my sister says,
and she *still* laughs at me.

I ask my mum,
"*Please* can I stay up early?"
My mum says *she's* tired
so *I* have to go to bed.

My mum's getting to be a pretty old mum.
She has a crumpled face when she smiles
and an old hairdo.

Years and years ago
when I was a tiny baby
I dreamed a witch was
chasing me.

She looked like my mum with a new hairdo.

DOOM!

Sometimes I dream about a fear-us tiger.
Flop! Floom! Doom!
He crashes right out of my curtains.

Even my sister has bad dreams
— about an evil wicked wolf.
Just like in *The Three Little Pigs*,
only more eviler.

My mum says there *is* such things
as fear-us tigers and witches
because dreams are real.
Dreams are more real
than bathtubs.
Dreams are more real
than houses.

My sister says I can stay up past bedtime
and watch the end of a cool movie with her.

She told me it was a *good* kids' movie, but it wasn't.
It was *Bloodsuckers From Mars.*

My mum leaves my frog lamp on
because I get scared in the dark.

But then my frog lamp glows in the dark
like a

Bloodsucker

from outer space.

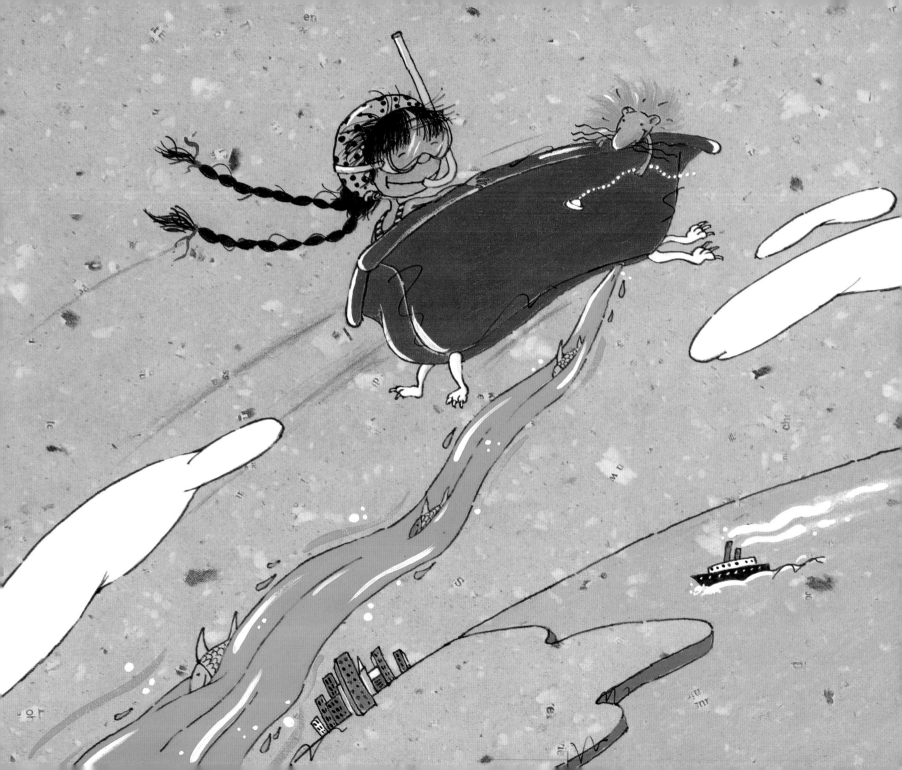

The night before I go in Grade One
I dream I am flying around the world
in a red bathtub.

When we fly over my new school,
Lion pulls the plug out.

CAW!

I have one good dream at least. It's about Pine-Cone.

Caw!   Caw!   Caw!

He's building a nest between my ears!

In the morning when I open my eyes a crow flies out.

My mum calls to me,
"Time to get dressed for school!"
"I'm pudding on my clothes," I call down to her.
"Get it? *Pudding* on my clothes?"

At breakfast my mum says to me,
"Eat your eggs they will give you strong legs."

But it's not easy to eat when you've got one gone tooth.

My mum and my sister drive me to Grade One.
I squeeze Lion tight when I go in the playground.

Some bullies say Lion looks like a bumish-colour,
but not to me.
He's a sunnish-looking colour.
To me.

My sister says bullies get angry
because they are sad inside.
My sister thinks *I* get angry,
but that's because *I'm* sad.
I want to break the whole world.
When I'm

SAD.

At recess I sing a song:
"All the kids hate me.
Oh, Mamma,
I hope you can pick me up early from school today."

All I see is home in my tiny little head.

At lunchtime I start having the best day
of my life.
I meet my best new friend Chelsea,
who has a stuffy named

SEAL.

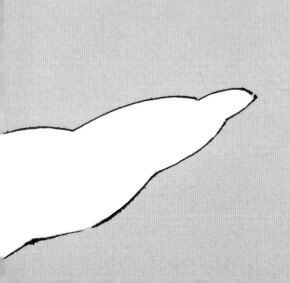

Tomorrow I am going to bring My Mum for Show and Tell.
I'll tell all my new friends,
"This is My Old Mum.
I got her when I was very small."

Then I am going to tell my friends
about the time Lion and me went flying
in a red bathtub
and a hot dog bit my head off
and Pine-Cone turned into a

CROW.

I'm
not
just
dreaming,
you
know.